Happy Hooves

Ta Dah!

For Reuben and Amabel.
A.B.

For Mum, who always helps me overcome
any obstacles I come up against.
R.E.

First published in 2014 by Fat Fox Books ltd

Fox's Den, Wickets, Frittenden Road, Staplehurst, Kent TN12 0DH.
www.fatfoxbooks.com

ISBN: 978-0992872816

Fat Fox and associated logos are trademarks and/or registered
trademarks of Fat Fox Books Ltd.

Text copyright © A. Bogie 2014.
Illustrations copyright © Rebecca Elliott 2014.

The right of A. Bogie to be identified as the author and Rebecca Elliott
to be identified as the illustrator of this work has been asserted.

A CIP catalogue record for this book is available from the British Library.

Printed and bound in China.

Happy Hooves
Ta Dah!

A. Bogie   Rebecca Elliott

fatfoxbooks.com

At the dawn of the day, with the sun's first ray,
A donkey awoke and gave a loud **bray.**

Across the hills in the morning light
Was a glimmer of ocean, just in sight.

The donkey called to his friends who lived near
And said 'I've had the greatest idea!

I dreamt of a jaunt to the sea and sand,
What a change of scene from this muddy land.'

'Today is the day, my dream is in reach,
   Let's have an adventure and go to the beach!'

   They set off together; a funny old crowd,
   All of the animals laughing out loud.

With happy hooves, the gang kept on walking
But what they saw next stopped them all talking.
Trembling and shaking the cow quickly hid,
For what lay ahead was a big cattle grid!

Five metal poles bridged a huge gap,
The cow insisted 'We must go back.'
'This won't defeat us,' the donkey declared,
'We can **jump over,** don't be scared.'

With a click of his heels, over he flew.
The cow's jaw dropped, could this be true?

'Ta Dah!' cried Donkey. 'I made it, you see
How easy it is to jump like me!'

'Oh,' said Sheep, 'it's not such a breeze
To leap up high with my knobbly knees.
But I shall try, as I heard a tale
Of a woolly sheep that crossed this trail.'

He lay on his side, and tucked in his hooves,
Rolled onto his back, and started to move.

'Ta Dah!' cried Sheep. 'I made it, you see
How easy it is to roll like me!'

'It's simple,' said Foal,
'when wrapped up in wool,
With my long legs, I'd look like a fool.
But have no fear, there was a story
Of a horse that danced across with glory.'

With that she sprung into the air,
And whirled and twirled, landing with flair!
'Ta Dah!' cried Foal. 'I made it, you see
How easy it is to jig like me!'

'**Oh no,**' said Pig, 'to cross like that
Is hard for me with my belly so fat!
But these round sides will give me style,
My special performance will make you smile.'

'I'll dip my head and bound into a vault,
I call it my **piggy somersault.**'

'**Ta Dah!**' cried Pig. 'I made it, you see
How easy it is to vault like me!'

'I cannot do it,' the cow mooed back,
'It's safer to stay this side of the track.'
The cow bowed her head, 'I can't cross the grate,
You must go now, or you'll be too late.'

Donkey brayed, 'All is not lost,
I've found a way for you to cross.
look over there, lodged in the hedge,
See that wood?

We'll make a ledge!'

The animals worked, heaving and tugging,
What a good team, pushing and lugging.
The bridge was complete, they all gave a cheer,

The cow stood grinning from ear to ear.

Clanking her bell, she started to stride,
Thinking how silly she'd been to hide!
'Ta Dah!' cried Cow. 'I made it, you see
How easy it is to stride like me.'

'At last we can head on our way,
Let's go to the beach. Hip! Hip! Hooray!'
On they marched, whistling a tune,
Down the path and over a dune.

They arrived and ran into the sea,

Splishing and splashing,
and laughing with glee.
They built a sandcastle with a big moat,
And used pretty shells to make a boat.

The sleepy sun stopped shining bright,
They all turned home, it would soon be night.
With smiles on their faces, they

lay down their heads.

And dreamed of the beach, whilst asleep in their beds.